Stop Bullying Now!

Respecting the Contributions of
Muslim Americans

Sloan MacRae

PowerKiDS
press

New York

Published in 2013 by The Rosen Publishing Group, Inc.
29 East 21st Street, New York, NY 10010

First Edition

Editor: Jennifer Way
Book Design: Erica Clendening and Ashley Drago
Layout Design: Andrew Povolny

Library of Congress Cataloging-in-Publication Data

MacRae, Sloan.
 Respecting the contributions of Muslim Americans / by Sloan MacRae. — 1st ed.
     p. cm. — (Stop bullying now!)
 Includes index.
 ISBN 978-1-4488-7444-6 (library binding) — ISBN 978-1-4488-7517-7 (pbk.) —
 ISBN 978-1-4488-7591-7 (6-pack)
 1. Muslims—United States—History. 2. Islam—United States—History. I. Title.
 E184.M88M33 2013
 305.6'97073—dc23

                                    2011049575

Manufactured in the United States of America

CPSIA Compliance Information: Batch #SW12PK: For Further Information contact Rosen Publishing, New York, New York at 1-800-237-9932

Contents

Bullying and Discrimination

Many Muslim Americans face **discrimination** from other Americans. Muslim American children are often bullied by other kids. Bullying and discrimination are wrong and often happen because people fear others who are different from them.

America is made up of people from many different cultures and of people who practice many different religions. Muslims practice a religion called **Islam**. Some people fear Muslims because of the Muslim **terrorists** who killed 3,000 Americans on a day known as 9/11. These terrorists were not Americans, and their beliefs are not those of Islam. Learning more about the different groups of people who have contributed to America's history builds understanding and respect for fellow Americans.

Muslim American kids are sometimes bullied at school because of their religion. Bullying often stems from ignorance and fear of people from different backgrounds.

What Is Bullying?

Bullying is making another person feel hurt or threatened through words or actions. Bullying can mean hitting a person or threatening to hurt a person. It could also mean calling someone names, spreading rumors, or excluding another person. Bullying can happen both face-to-face and online.

Bullying often goes on for a long period of time. ▼

A bullied student may feel lonely, unhappy, or afraid.

Bullies often pick on people they see as different. A Muslim American boy who goes to a school where there are not many other Muslim Americans might be bullied because he is seen as different. Bullying is wrong. No one deserves to be bullied. Teachers, parents, or other trusted adults can help if you or someone at your school is being bullied.

Islam began in the year 622 with a **prophet** named Muhammad. Muhammad believed that Allah, or God, spoke to him and gave him new laws that people must follow. These laws are gathered in the **Koran**, which is Islam's holy book.

Today, more than one billion people all over the world practice Islam. Different Muslim groups practice different beliefs and follow different levels of strictness. Most Muslims do not eat pork or drink **alcohol**. The two biggest Muslim groups are Sunni and Shia. The United States has more people of the different branches of Islam living together than any other country in the world.

Depending on which branch of Islam they follow and how strictly they follow it, Muslim women may cover their hair and neck. They may also cover their faces or wear garments over their clothes when they are in public.

Muslims in America

Some Muslim American families have lived in the United States for generations. Nearly two-thirds of all Muslim Americans **immigrated** to the United States, though. Muslim Americans have come to the United States from the Middle East, Africa, Asia, and Europe. Islam is the world's second-biggest religion after Christianity.

The Islamic Center of America, shown here, is in Dearborn, Michigan. It is the largest mosque, or Islamic house of worship, in North America.

Like other families, Muslim American families balance embracing everyday American life with teaching their children about their religious and cultural traditions.

Some Muslim Americans **converted** to Islam. This means they did not grow up as Muslims, but they decided later in life to practice Islam. Many famous Americans, like the boxer Muhammad Ali and Congressman Keith Ellison, have converted to Islam. Thousands of Muslims are born into Muslim families and grow up practicing Islam.

Muslim soldiers are recorded as having fought in some of the American Revolution's most famous battles, such as the Battle of Lexington, shown here.

Groups of Muslims have been coming to the United States throughout the country's history. Historians guess that at least 40,000 of the people brought to America from Africa to be slaves were Muslim. Records also show that there were soldiers with Muslim names on the lists of people who fought in the American Revolution.

The Founding Father Thomas Jefferson believed that America should provide religious freedom for all citizens. Religious freedom is guaranteed by the **Constitution**. The Constitution is the document that sets up the form of the United States' government.

Hadji Ali (1828–1902)

Monument to Hadji Ali

Hadji Ali was born in what is now the country of Jordan. He came to America in 1856 to train camels in the Arizona desert for the Army's new US Camel Corps. The Camel Corps experiment failed, but "Hi Jolly," as he was nicknamed, stayed in the United States for the rest of his life.

Here is Ali after receiving the Presidential Medal of Freedom. It is given to people who make special contributions to America and to world peace. It is one of the highest honors a citizen can receive.

Cassius Clay was born in 1942 in Louisville, Kentucky. This was during a time when African Americans did not have the same **civil rights** as white Americans. Clay grew up facing bullying and discrimination. As an adult, he became a heavyweight-boxing champion. In 1964, Clay changed his name to Muhammad Ali. In 1975, he converted to Islam.

After retiring from boxing in 1981, Ali focused on **humanitarian** causes. In 2005, he received the Presidential Medal of Freedom for this work. He has traveled the world promoting peace, civil rights, education, and programs to end hunger. Ali's career both inside and outside the ring have earned him the nickname the Greatest.

AHMET ERTEGÜN
(1923–2006)

Ahmet Ertegün was born in Istanbul, Turkey, and came to America in 1935. As a boy, he fell in love with music. He founded Atlantic Records in 1947. Ertegün discovered, signed, and produced some of the greatest artists in rock-and-roll history. Atlantic Records remains one of the world's biggest record labels.

Ahmed Zewail

Ahmed Zewail was born in Egypt in 1946. He came to the United States to study at the University of Pennsylvania in 1972. He has been a professor of physics and chemistry at the California Institute of Technology since 1976. In 1982, he became a US citizen.

Zewail also advises President Obama on policy matters related to science.

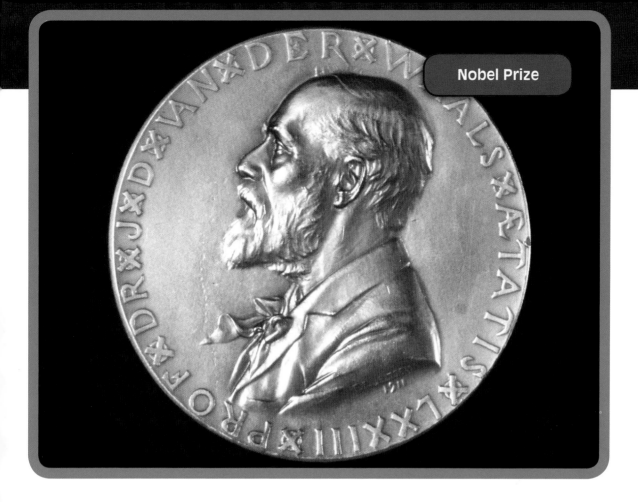

Zewail's work in chemistry has helped scientists better understand how matter works. He won the Nobel Prize in Chemistry in 1999. In 2010, President Barack Obama named Zewail a science envoy. In this role, he travels to Muslim-majority countries in the Middle East to promote cooperation between the United States and those countries in scientific and technological projects.

These Muslim American girls are at a rally in New York City held to show support for Muslim Americans' rights.

On September 11, 2001, a small group of terrorists killed 3,000 Americans. The events of that day are now known as 9/11. The terrorists were Muslims, and now many Americans believe that all Muslims are terrorists. It is important not to confuse the beliefs of a few with those of a whole group.

Muslim Americans have faced greater discrimination since 9/11. They are sometimes singled out for extra screening at airport **security**. People sometimes say or write hateful things about Muslims or **vandalize** their homes or mosques. Muslim American children are often bullied at school.

Fareed Zakaria
(1964–)

Fareed Zakaria was born in India in 1964 and became a US citizen in 2000. Zakaria is a journalist who has written for *Time* and *Newsweek* and hosts a television show on CNN. Zakaria has often reported on America's relationships with Muslim-majority countries in the Middle East and how they affect world events.

Keith Ellison

Keith Ellison was born in Michigan in 1963. He was raised Roman Catholic and converted to Islam at age 19. In 2006, he became the first Muslim American ever elected to the House of Representatives. He represents part of Minnesota. When politicians are sworn into office, most carry Bibles with them. Instead of a Bible, Ellison carried a Koran that was once owned by Thomas Jefferson.

Here is Ellison (center) making a speech in Washington, D.C., in 2011.

Ellison was not only the first Muslim American elected to Congress. He was also the first African American to represent Minnesota in Congress.

In 2007, the American-Arab Anti-Discrimination Committee awarded Ellison its Trailblazer Award for his work promoting peace and civil rights. In 2010, Ellison was elected to his third term in Congress, where he proudly serves his state and country.

Muslim Americans Deserve Your Respect

America has always been a land of different people living and working together. It may be challenging to get along, but it does not excuse bullying or discrimination.

We should never fear or hate a group of people. If your friends or family members say bad things about Muslim Americans, you should remind them that all Americans are equal. Understanding that all Americans have the same rights helps you have respect for everyone.

Everyone is different, but understanding one another breaks down fear and builds respect.

Glossary

alcohol (AL-kuh-hol) A liquid, such as beer or wine, that can make a person lose control or get drunk.

civil rights (SIH-vul RYTS) The rights that citizens have.

Constitution (kon-stih-TOO-shun) The basic rules by which the United States is governed.

converted (kun-VERT-ed) Changed from one faith to another.

discrimination (dis-krih-muh-NAY-shun) Treating a person badly or unfairly just because he or she is different.

humanitarian (hyoo-ma-nuh-TER-ee-un) Having to do with making things better for people.

immigrated (IH-muh-grayt-ed) Moved to another country to live.

Islam (IS-lom) A faith based on the teachings of Muhammad and the Koran.

Koran (kuh-RAN) The holy book of Islam.

prophet (PRAH-fet) Someone who says he or she brings messages from God.

security (sih-KYUR-ih-tee) Safety or freedom from danger.

terrorists (TER-er-ists) People or groups that seek to scare or threaten with violence illegally.

vandalize (VAN-duh-lyz) To damage or ruin another person's property.

Index

Websites

Due to the changing nature of Internet links, PowerKids Press has developed an online list of websites related to the subject of this book. This site is updated regularly. Please use this link to access the list:
www.powerkidslinks.com/sbn/muslim/